Dedicated to

David and Albertress Stearns

and

The Shain and Blance Families

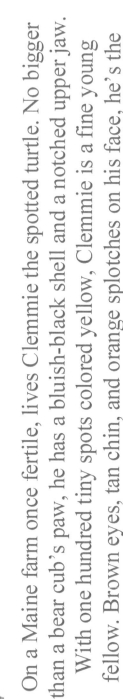

On a Maine farm once fertile, lives Clemmie the spotted turtle. No bigger than a bear cub's paw, he has a bluish-black shell and a notched upper jaw. With one hundred tiny spots colored yellow, Clemmie is a fine young fellow. Brown eyes, tan chin, and orange splotches on his face, he's the cutest little turtle around the whole place.

Because his species is endangered, Clemmie is surrounded by lots of strangers. Since his mom went missing the autumn before, Clemmie now lives by an old cow pond, not far from shore. Gone are the farm's former dwellers, who left nothing behind, but shadowy woods and mossy stone cellars.

Once, a cruel raven revealed, a story that made Clemmie's heart race and reel. Clemmie's mom the fox did kill, supposedly, just for the thrill. Clemmie can't go far walking, since the fox might be stalking. In every nook and every cranny, Clemmie knows where to hide, for when the fox goes outside. You see, predators are always hunting prey, especially for little turtles to slay. With no memories of other family to keep, Clemmie hangs his head and tries not to weep.

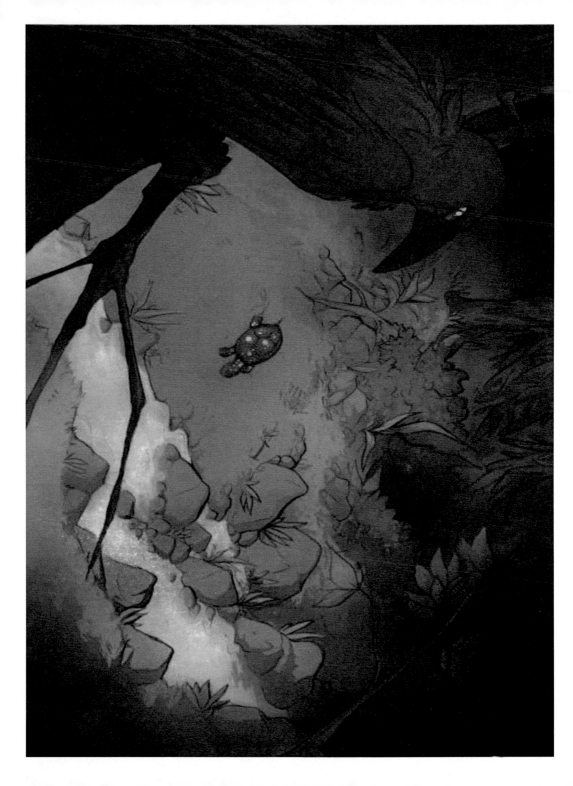

In the middle of the pond where the sun still shines, is a small island covered with vines. On its low highland, a seed was once sown, which freed an apple tree now fully grown. Naughty crows caw about the tree's tasty fruits, and the scrumptious angleworms living in its roots. Clemmie yearns for the island and its wonderful bounty—some say the best in all of Penobscot County. Alas, Clemmie never learned to swim, and his chances of reaching the island were very slim.

Every day, Clemmie must find something to eat, preferably a bug with a morsel of meat. Unfortunately, food is lacking, so there's never time for slacking. Foraging in the thicket, he might find a juicy cricket, but mostly, it's just hairy spiders that taste nothing like sweet cider. And, when Clemmie gets thirsty, he accepts his own dare, and goes down to the water with the greatest of care.

Eventually, the long summer waned, and the approaching autumn gained. Warm days flew fast, and cold nights seemed to last. After the first morning frost, bugs became few, and Clemmie's hunger grew and grew.

One morning, as his tummy rumbled, into the pond an apple tumbled. For much of the day, gentle breezes blew to and fro, as if the Macintosh didn't know which way to go. Just when watching became a real chore, the prized apple washed ashore. Though it was bruised and battered, for Clemmie it did not matter. So sweet and nutritious, the apple was delicious.

Soon, Clemmie lost track of time, and darkness started to climb. He scurried to get back, before the fox could attack. Regrettably, outside Clemmie's earthen lair, the terrible fox glared. So startled by the sight, Clemmie stayed hidden throughout the night. Retreating into his shell and not making a peep, after a while, he fell asleep.

His head hurting from a sudden waking, Clemmie felt a vicious shaking.
Sharp teeth gnashed and gnawed, because he was trapped in the fox's maw.
In his mind, thoughts ran manic, and inside his shell, Clemmie panicked.
Waiting anxiously for the coming calm, Clemmie cried for his lost mom.

Unexpected visions came instead, of bittersweet memories, Clemmie thought long dead. Him and his mom basking on a log, happily listening to a bullfrog…digging under slimy rocks, eating wriggling grubs until their bellies popped…wading in a shallow streambed, never imagining such awful dread. When Clemmie thought of what he'd forgotten, wild anger was suddenly begotten. So emboldened by these remembrances, his fear was no longer a hindrance.

With a bite that was wicked fierce, the fox's tongue the turtle did pierce. From a hurt he could not help, the fox let out a big yelp. Through the air, Clemmie went flying, dropping into the pond without even trying. So fearful of a drowning death, Clemmie took a deep breath.

Many anxious minutes passed by, before Clemmie realized he would not die. You see, turtles need not fret, if they get wet. Sticking his head out and looking about, the first thing he saw was a pretty brook trout. In the water, which was crystal clear, Clemmie felt very good cheer. Though above the surface of the pond it was chilly autumn, he found it much warmer on the bottom.

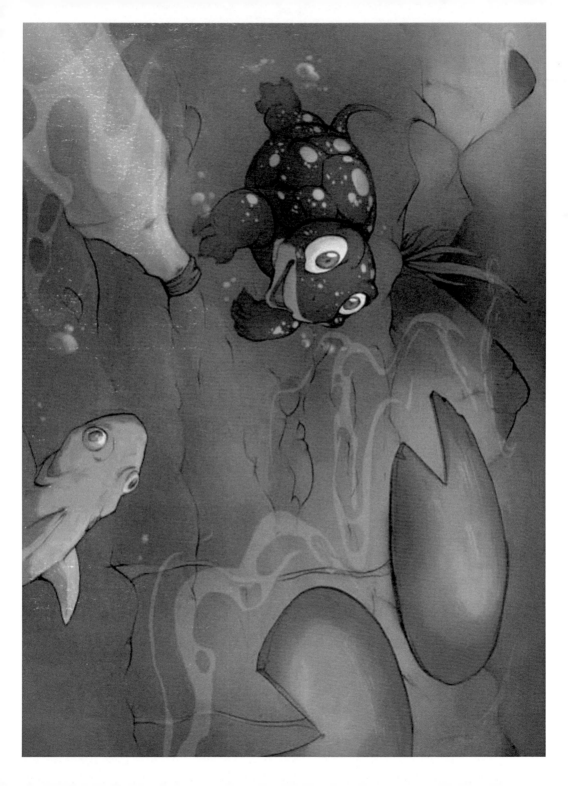

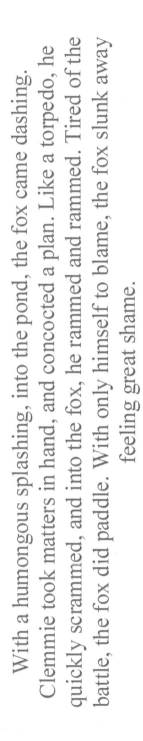

With a humongous splashing, into the pond, the fox came dashing. Clemmie took matters in hand, and concocted a plan. Like a torpedo, he quickly scrammed, and into the fox, he rammed and rammed. Tired of the battle, the fox did paddle. With only himself to blame, the fox slunk away feeling great shame.

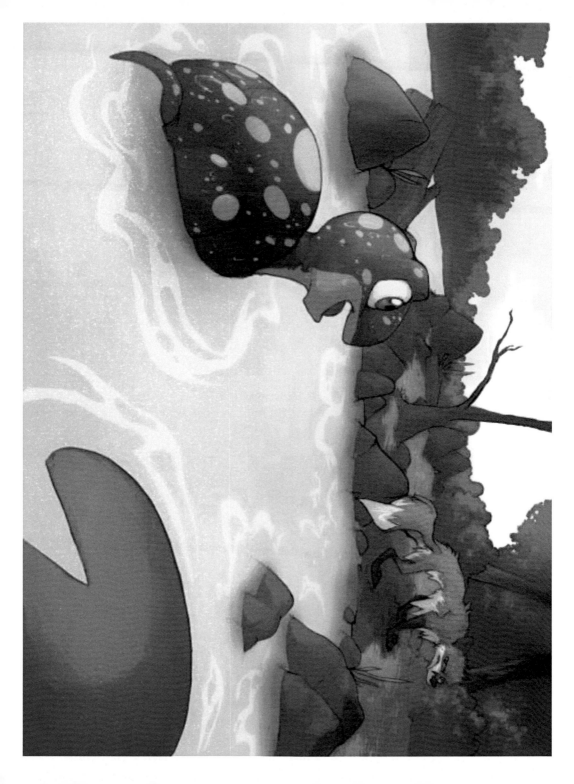

Surfacing into the light, Clemmie swam with all of his might. The island no longer distant, he arrived in nearly an instant. Clemmie ate apples galore, until his belly could hold no more. He dug a hole, and inside he squeezed, before the ground completely freezed. Not long after, the little turtle slept, with lovely memories that he kept.

At last, spring came dawning, and Clemmie awoke and started yawning. After a long winter slumber, Clemmie could barely lumber, but as soon as he was fitter, he did not fritter. On his new island, Clemmie did toil, digging for fat angleworms in the rich soil. He ate until he was done, and lounged all afternoon in the warm sun.

When summer solstice finally came, another spotted turtle did the same. Clemmie was as happy as bright sunshine, when she said her name was Clementine.